Generics

Generics

JULIE ZHOU

Book design by Natalie Eilbert
Cover art: "Grounded" © 2018 Justine Szafran
Published by Gold Line Press
http://goldlinepress.com
Gold Line titles are distributed by Small Press Distribution
This title is also available for purchase directly from the publisher
www.spdbooks.org : 800.869.7553

Library of Congress Cataloging-in-Publication Data
Generics : Julie Zhou
Library of Congress Control Number 2015942420
Zhou, Julie
ISBN 978-1-938900-28-2

Contents

To AB, JG, BT, EK, KP, EC, KZ, AD, AZ, CM, NH, SK.

For the women who have taught me fire and grit, honesty and grace, strength and longing—who have given me a spine made of steel and the courage to imagine new worlds. I will never, *never* know how to thank you enough.

ONE

WHEN YOU ARE FOUR, you leave your grandparents' apartment in Shanghai to live with your parents in a shoebox apartment on the University of Wisconsin's graduate campus. Your parents feel like strangers until the day they start to tell you stories before bed and you recognize in your dad's voice the same measured certainty, the same lilting rhythm as your grandmother has.

Your first word in Chinese was moon, *yue*, for the tiny crescent-shaped cookies your grandmother made you for breakfast every day. In English, you start with mama and dad and then numbers, the ten-digits of your parents' shared cell phone. When it is your dad's night to sit with you, he reads from an anthology of lectures by Richard Feynman, so that you learn the alphabet as a set of variables: quadratics and theorems and sets of axes. He tells you one day that he almost named you Arline after Richard Feynman's wife, and you scrunch your nose and make a face. He pokes at the wrinkle it makes between your eyebrows until you laugh and it disappears.

Your mom works the night shift on weekdays, but on Saturdays, she's all yours. On those nights, she sits on the edge of your bed and braids your hair into two neat plaits and tells you about princesses and dragons and towers and curses. She favors the originals— though you don't know this until you're much older—and so your "Little Mermaid" isn't redheaded and brazen, but is voiceless and martyred, and your "Sleeping Beauty" is a warning about women who don't listen to the rules.

She prefers the ones that aren't about princesses: Little Red Riding Hood, The Little Match Girl, Peter Pan, and The Emperor's New

Clothes. But one night in May, she tells you about a little girl named "Cinder-Ella" and her selfish stepsisters and her wicked stepmother and you hate them, hate them up until the very end when you are almost asleep and your mom is finishing the story and she tells you that you should dream of the stepmother and the things that made her cruel. The things that made her angry. The things that broke her heart.

"We're all made of something," she whispers against your cheek. "We all hurt. Even the villains." She smiles and stands, turning out the light as she leaves. She smooths a hand across her stomach, round and silhouetted in the doorway. "She was a mom too."

You fall asleep wondering what it would be like to be wicked. You wonder if you would still love your mother if she were like that; if she would still love you.

The next week, you ask her for another story about the wicked stepmother. She laughs, tells you that she'll think about it while you brush your teeth and you hug her stomach and sprint to the bathroom. When you come back, she's in the rocking chair next to your bed. She tucks you in and turns the lights down and presses a kiss to your forehead.

"This one is called 'Snow White,'" she says, smoothing a hand across your back as you settle in. "It's about a stepmother, but it's about a princess, too. A lost princess."

So she tells you about a girl with lips as red as a rose and skin as white as snow and hair as dark as a crow's wing, and a castle on a cliffside and a magic mirror and a lovely little cottage with seven dwarves. She tells you about desperation and loneliness and a queen who wants to be the most beautiful woman in the world, about enchanted combs and lace bodices and jealousy so dark it turns an apple to poison.

"And when she returned to the castle and asked the magic

mirror—'mirror, mirror, on the wall, who's the fairest of them all?' It replied 'you, my queen, are fairest of them all.'"

Your mom gasps and you think that it's part of the story until she yells for your dad, her hands palepalepale in the dimly lit room, gripping the handles of the rocking chair. Your dad sprints in and then it's all a blur: your mom bundled into the car. Your babysitter telling you to wave goodbye, that you'll have a new sister soon. You, waiting and waiting for your mom to come back to finish the story about the sad queen and the lonely castle and the poisoned apple.

MIRROR, MIRROR
(A BIPARTITE FAIRYTALE)

...AND SO, AS THOSE IN LOVE *are wont to do, the prince and the princess were married. In the third year of their marriage, the princess gave birth to a baby girl, with her mother's eyes and her mother's smile and her father's crooked right toe. They named her Sara, and they lived blissfully for nine years, until a plague blew through the kingdom and took the princess with it.*

....

The evening after her mom's funeral, with the reception still in full swing, Sara slipped into her parents' closet with a photo album: the one her mom had started putting together for her service when she found out the cancer was terminal.

"I'd like to choose, a little bit, how people remember me," she'd told Sara's father when he tried to tell her she shouldn't work too hard. "I think it might be too late for me to work myself to death, you know." She'd laughed, lighthearted and lovely, and Sara's dad had looked both charmed and desperately sad.

She'd asked Sara to help in the last few weeks, when she left the hospital and came home to stay until the end. Sara would run home from the bus stop, flop breathlessly onto her parents' bed, and they'd rifle through albums together as Sara picked her favorites. The best one was a school portrait of her mom at ten years old, curls smoothed back into a red headband, a closed-mouth smile because she'd lost a tooth just before portrait day and was "gap-toothed as all hell." It was Sara's favorite of the favorites—because in the right light, if she squinted, it was just like looking in a mirror.

She tucked herself in the dusty shadows between her mom's old dresses, breathed in the familiar scent of lavender and cloves, and paged through the rest of the album slowly, carefully. The last picture in the book was a Polaroid from her mom's college graduation, her hair sun-gilded and tangled in the wind, her smile full of bright hope. Underneath, in her mom's tidy script, it said—Northwestern University, 3/18. "Nothing gold can stay."

. . . .

And so the prince became king and the king was still father; and when he looked at his bright, brave daughter, all he could see was her mother, taken too young. He resolved to find a new wife: not a princess but a queen, to rule at his side, with her feet planted so firmly in the ground that she'd never stand to be blown away.

. . . .

Her stepmother moved in the day after Sara's birthday, with five suitcases and a parakeet named Faberge. She smiled at Sara, a slow, knowing smile. Her name was Penelope.

"Call me Penny. Everyone does."

It seemed such an unexpectedly clumsy name for the slim, suit-clad woman standing in the doorway that Sara stumbled over the greeting she'd practiced in the mirror, graceful and aloof.

"It's a plea—I'm happy to—It's a pleasure to welcome you to our home, Penny." The name felt foreign on her tongue and Sara resisted the urge to say it again, just to see if repetition would make it better.

"It's nice to meet you, sweetheart." Her voice was low, smooth—molasses on a knife's edge. "I've heard nothing but wonderful things."

She brushed a kiss across Sara's cheek and the cool press of her lips felt like a warning.

. . . .

The daughter became princess and the queen became stepmother, and the castle began to change.

. . . .

The days after were less a warning than a paradigm shift. The pantry was stripped and the freezer emptied and they handed in their family card at Costco for a membership at the local gym instead. There were new shoes in the entryway and new coats in the closet and a new voice when Sara got home from school.

"Are you sure you want to eat that, honey?"

"That sweater—it just isn't doing any favors for your figure."

"Small bites; ladylike, sweetheart."

Sara learned to bury hunger when she was in the kitchen making a sandwich during her stepmother's book club and overheard a woman telling her she was lucky to have inherited such a beautiful daughter.

"Yes," her stepmother had laughed. "She really is a pretty thing. It's a pity she's so chubby." Something caught in Sara's throat, ugly and sour. "Not my genes though," Penny said.

The rest of the conversation faded to a dull roar and Sara felt her cheeks warm as she padded quietly out of the kitchen. She left her sandwich on the cutting board, crusts neatly cut off.

. . . .

The king buried himself in the kingdom, but the queen, beautiful and proud—no less the first because of the second—was a ruler in her own right; and she gave herself no rest, day or night in this new kingdom until she had found a purpose, a project. She found it in her new daughter, who still let loneliness and yearning and passion show on her face just as earnestly as a child in the cradle.

"I can teach you control," the queen said. "I can teach you how to be less. Be less, or this world will want more, more and more until they have worn you away," warned the queen, beautiful and proud and no less lonely than the girl-princess.

. . . .

Sara started to count calories for something to do in the choreographed silence of their new family dinners. Asparagus with lemon: 110 calories. Sweet potato mash with a teaspoon of butter: 385 calories. Her mom's favorite chocolate chip cookies: 192 calories. Penny smiled at her the first day she said no to dessert, and when she turned down a second helping of lasagna the next night, Penny rested a hand on her shoulder and asked her if she'd like to go shopping for new clothes.

"Always dress like you're going to see your worst enemy," Penny advised the next day, as she parked in front of the mall. When she stepped out of the car, her stilettos clicked against the sidewalk, as precise as a metronome. Sara caught a glimpse of their reflections in the department store doors: Penny impossibly slim and straight-backed in a silk pantsuit, and Sara, hair askew, bundled in one of her dad's old sweaters.

My worst enemy, she thought.

. . . .

The princess stayed kind and gentle, thoughtful and generous, but pride grew higher and higher in her heart like a weed, until it settled as longing: for her stepmother's approval, for her father's recognition, for her mother's face in the mirror. "Be less," she told herself every night. "Be less."

. . . .

The math started to escalate until it wasn't about an obsession with the numbers anymore, the tidiness of counting. Instead, Sara started to measure in relativities. Too many calories. More than yesterday. Eat half as much tomorrow. On good days, on days that she felt like she'd eaten little enough for a reward, Sara would page through Penny's coffee table magazines and cut out the people that she wished she could look like: glossy, airbrushed slips of paper that she tacked above her desk, layers upon layers, so many that they began to look like a jabberwocky collection of limbs.

But the real wish was the worn picture tucked under Sara's pillow: the last picture she had of her mom: 29, slim and bird-boned, her nose crinkled in a half-laugh. It was one of the rare pictures of her alone, and it was partially for this reason that Sara cherished it. Sometimes, she pretended that it wasn't her mom, but that it was her future self: young and beautiful and happy.

"You look so much like your mother."

"Has anyone ever told you that you have your mom's eyes?"

"You are just like a miniature version of your mother; gonna grow up to be a looker."

In the mirror, Sara looked for her mom every morning: in her forehead, in the set of her jaw, the shape of her nose. On great days, on days that she felt pretty, she'd pull her hair into the high, loose bun that her mom liked to wear, wayward strands of hair against her cheekbones.

She wondered sometimes who she had left to be after she grew into that last picture of her mother. If she'd know how to recognize herself.

. . . .

The longing seeped from the princess's heart to her bones, heavy and heavier, until it grew too much for her to hold on her own. From her lady-in-waiting, she learned of a witch who could make such problems disappear with a potion and a wave of her wand. So one evening, when the king and queen were busy preparing for a ball, she slipped away with her mother's necklace and her father's signet ring tucked in the folds of her cloak.

. . . .

The kids at school called it "Wonderland," the tiny antique store tucked away at the end of the boardwalk, the one with the porthole windows and creaking floors. Its real name was "The Glass Menagerie," the wooden letters swinging over the door, paint flaking off to drift onto the shoulders of any intrepid customers. Danny Gupta had stolen the "G and the "L" from the sign one Halloween—the next day, they'd been replaced with letters just as weather-worn and dull, the only proof they'd ever been stolen sitting on the edge of Danny's nightstand table.

The store itself was home to a specific set of odds and ends: tarnished mirrors and sand-smoothed bottles and stained glass windows fogged with age. It was a living mosaic, where you could buy baubles by the crate and sea glass by the pound— and where if you knew the right way to ask, you could get your palms read for five dollars and a dream catcher for fifty cents and an alternative pharmacy for a couple twenties and a good story.

. . . .

The princess walked into the witch's cottage through the front door because that's how she was raised; falling down rabbit holes was for the graceless, fairy dust was for cheaters, and stepping through looking glasses would be disastrously impolite for a guest to do.

. . . .

The bell over the door rang, a sad, tired chime. The store was empty.

Sara wrapped her hands in the folds of her dress, finger-shaped bruises up and down her arm. They'd started appearing every time she showered or sat down too suddenly, but part of her thought they were pretty, these purple-dark constellations.

"Hello?"

Her feet sent a flurry of dust wafting before her and it hung, suspended in silty, strange sunlight until she took another step. The store felt like a hallucination, like being trapped inside a kaleidoscope.

"Hello?"

There was a rustle in the back of the store and a dark-haired young woman stepped into the doorway. She was dressed all in black, inky and cashmere-soft, the kind of black you could fall into and never wake up from. When she walked, it was with a cat's lazy grace, liquid and slow. She looked, Sara thought absently, like a shadow.

"Can I help you?" the woman said, moving towards the counter.

Sara smoothed her hands over her dress self-consciously, clearing her throat. She wanted to say that the reflection in the mirror had started to hate her, that she was looking for something that would make her look like her mom; that she just wanted to be good enough, golden enough. That she wanted Penny to love her and her dad to just see her. But instead she repeated the words that Bella Hastings told her to say when she'd told her about Wonderland, after she caught Sara with her fingers down her throat in the girls' bathroom during lunch.

"I got these ephedrine tablets there and I dropped ten pounds in, like, three days," she'd said, with the frenetic earnestness of an addict. "It was better than the stomach flu." She'd rested a bird-boned hand on Sara's shoulder. "Trust me."

. . . .

The princess gave her hand to the witch.

"What might someone like you want here?" The witch smiled mischievously for a moment, and the princess was suddenly struck by how young she was. "Good things, pretty things, a looking-glass for your wall?" She extended a fist and opened her hand, two shadowy figures spinning just above her palm, writhing and intertwined. "A lost love? They call me the queen of hearts, you know."

"Only if your good things will make me good, and your looking-glass will make me beautiful and your lost love can bring back my mother," the princess replied somberly.

"And what will you give for that?" The witch touched the ring on the princess's finger. "The favor of a royal?" She lifted the necklace at the princess's neck. "Gold?" she said mockingly. She dropped the necklace. "Just trinkets."

"Everything," the princess said quietly. "I would give everything."

. . . .

"Care to hear a story?" Sara's words came out as a tremor, but the woman smiled and nodded.

"I'm Zelda." She stuck out her hand to shake Sara's.

"Alice."

Zelda snorted. "Sure it is." She pulled back a curtain and waved

Sara through. "Come on back."

The air in the storeroom was stale and thick with marijuana and incense, the room cluttered with boxes of mirrors and dusty boudoir tables. Zelda opened a cupboard with pockmarked glass doors, the shelves lined with pill bottles. Someone had lined them up in rainbow order, and Sara smiled a little as Zelda turned to her.

"So. Alice in Wonderland. What's your poison?"

. . . .

The princess buried herself in smoke and mirrors and the queen, beautiful and proud and no less likely to make mistakes for it, realized that a person was not a purpose and a daughter was not a project.

. . . .

Penny left quietly.

She handed Sara's father the divorce papers as if they were a two-week notice. "I can't stay in a house where everyone is living for a ghost."

She took her stilettos and her pantsuits and Faberge's cage and when she looked at Sara, there was something still and resigned flattening the air between them.

"Take care of yourself. You're getting a little thin." She brushed a hand over Sara's curls. It felt like an apology. Penny opened her mouth, then snapped it shut, jaw clenching for a moment before she spoke again. "You don't have to be your mother's daughter, you know." She leaned down to brush her lips across Sara's cheek, her voice as soft as an echo. "You don't have to be anyone's."

She left behind two silk slips, a single black heel, and Sara, fading at the edges. Her father called a therapist two weeks later, when he'd finally pulled himself out of the remnants of his marriage and saw Sara, brittle and small, his daughter shrinking to nothing. In the days that followed, Sara wondered if what it took for her dad to see her was just for her to stop looking like her mom.

. . . .

The little mermaid gave herself to the tides so that she could live near the shore, and the twelve dancing princesses buried their shoes in the earth and Rapunzel left her tower in the sky to touch the ground again. So the princess, too, came back to the surface.

. . . .

"So tell me a little about yourself," said the therapist, steepling his fingers under his chin, peering at her over wire-rimmed frames. There were a few crumbs caught in his beard, from lunch, perhaps, Sara thought; and not for the first time, she wondered if anyone had ever told him he looked a little bit like a wizard. He cleared his throat. "Tell me about your family."

Sara wanted to tell him about her mom: her voice and her smile and her golden-bright hair, how she took up all the oxygen in the room until everyone else was a little breathless. About Penny: about book clubs and shopping trips, about the sound of her heels on tile and the startled, hiccupping way that she'd laugh, the only messy thing about her. About her dad: about silence, about grief, about the hollowed out spaces that people leave behind.

But she didn't say any of it. Not yet.

Instead, she told him about the crippling fear that she wouldn't grow up to look like her mom. She told him that anorexia was like an archeological dig, patching something together from all the bits of bone she could find, trying to make something whole again. Trying to find another body's memories.

And then, when it felt like she had no more words left to give, she cleared her throat, twisting her necklace between her fingers. "My dad used to start every story he told about my mom with 'happily ever after.'"

TWO

YOU AND YOUR DAD TAKE your sister to the aquarium when she's three months old, for her first big outing. Your dad tucks her into a little red onesie, the one that your mom's business partner sent over when she was born. There are little felt ears and the sleeves fold over into padded mittens. Your dad bops her on the nose as he straps her into the car seat next to you.

Lyddie is quiet the entire drive—but she was born quiet, really. Chubby and dimpled, with long-lashed, serious eyes and a crop of wild black hair. She could focus on things a few days after she was born, could track your finger back and forth, and would fall asleep if you tried to play peek-a-boo. Your dad said once that she was an old soul in a young body, and your mom had smiled, wan and tired, smoothing a hand absently across Lyddie's back. You wondered for a little while if your dad meant that Lyddie had stolen your mom's soul, but when you asked your dad, he'd looked so stricken that you never asked again.

It's been three months and your mom has grown so thin that you overheard your grandma whispering to your grandpa that your mom was going to just fade to nothing if she stayed—and then she uses a word you don't know, *tante*, a word with sharp edges you aren't used to hearing in the rolling hills and valleys of the dialect they speak. You ask your grandma later and she explains to you that it's like the nerves you get before piano concerts, but not just nerves, not quite. It's something dark lurking in the corners of your soul, dragging you back to the spirit world. Like a haunting, she says.

So when your first grade teacher, Ms. Libby, asks you if your mom will be coming to parent-teacher conferences, you tell her that she can't, because she's haunted. You think it makes your mom sound special, chosen; but Ms. Libby pulls your dad aside when he comes to pick you up that day, her face kind and concerned.

He holds your hand as you walk to the parking lot, and explains that you shouldn't talk about problems at home to strangers.

"But it's Ms. Libby," you explain as you climb into the car. "She's not a stranger."

He helps you buckle. "Yes, but Ms. Libby isn't part of our family. So it's better not to tell her things that are just about our family, okay?" He kneels to look at you. "Like a secret. Can you keep a secret?"

You want to ask him what's wrong with your mom; why she isn't like your friend Amanda's mom, who has Amanda's baby brother permanently attached to her hip; or like your classmate Emmett's, who packs his lunchbox with little notes like "I love you!" and "Have a great day!" You want to ask him why she doesn't like to hold Lyddie; why she doesn't tell you stories anymore. You want to ask when she's going to come back to be your mom again.

But he looks sad, so you nod. "Yes."

He kisses your head. "Good girl."

When you get home from school, you go upstairs and crawl next to your mom in bed. She's watching *The Sound of Music* on mute, and the actors, mid-musical number, all seem distorted and cartoonish without their voices. You know, even without asking, that she's been watching it since you left her in the morning, because that's what she's done almost every day since she and Lyddie came home from the hospital: just watched *The Sound of Music* over and over again.

Sometimes late at night, on the way to the bathroom, you hear the click of the VCR rewinding, pale blue light flickering from under your parent's door.

She doesn't look down until you curl into her side, blinking at you blearily as if she can't quite see you.

"Hi, honey. How was school?"

You chatter about your classmates and your teacher and how you're learning about the solar system this week, until you turn and realize that your mom has fallen asleep, propped up against a pillow. You turn the TV off and close the door quietly, padding downstairs to join your dad in the kitchen, where he's feeding Lyddie mashed carrots.

"Can I help? She's asleep again."

He nods, murmurs a quiet "thank you," and hands you the spoon. "A couple bites, okay? I'm going to go check on your mom."

Lyddie gurgles as your dad goes upstairs, smacking her hands against her high chair, and you love her so, so much, your perfect little sister.

"I hope you learn how to talk soon," you tell her as you feed her a spoonful of carrot. "I'm going to tell you all the stories." She reaches for you with a chubby fist and smiles as if she's agreeing. You wipe an orange smudge from her cheek. "We're just waiting for mama to wake up. She tells the best ones."

THRILLER (WHITE)

I WAS IN A WHITE ROOM when they took him from me.

I remember because it was the kind of cruel, merciless white that makes you feel like pollution. The kind that stretches sticky fingers to your eyelids, and pries them apart so that you have to watch.

Those first hours, the pain folded me in half. My water broke, spots of blood speckling the marble tiles. I kept bleeding as they called the paramedics and I kept bleeding when the ambulance came and they got me to the hospital so fast that I don't even remember the drive. Just the pain. Just the blood. Just holding him in.

They wheeled me into that white white room and laid me on my side on the bed.

The needle was cool against my spine, the anesthesiologist's hands folding over my back, assured and vaguely orange-scented. Then a tingle in my hips, in my pelvic bones—the ilium and ischium, I'd learned in college anatomy—numbness creeping its way to my feet until I felt like a body divided.

They told me I should eat, that I wasn't fully dilated yet and the contractions were regular, and I should keep my strength up. So a nurse brought a little white tray with a turkey sandwich, a limp salad dressed in dark vinegar, and a little dish of canned peaches floating in syrup. I looked at those peaches as she left, gold and glistening against the white plastic of the bowl, and suddenly all I wanted was a ripe summer peach from my parents' farm. I could almost feel it; the downy skin against my lips, the slick-sweet flesh underneath, juice dripping down my chin, my neck, my collarbone, sticking my shirt to my skin.

I ate my turkey sandwich and my peach cup, the syrup thick and cloying, stuck to the back of my throat. And then I settled in with the infomercial channel and counted the contractions and called Robert. Called my mom. Called to buy a waffle iron with eight interchangeable plates; hung up when I remembered I'd left my wallet at the office.

I wasn't due for another three weeks so Robert was in Hong Kong at a software conference. He'd bought a plane ticket immediately when I called, and my mom was flying in from San Francisco, but for those first hours it was just me and Cole. *Donghai*, my parents suggested, for his Chinese name. After my great-grandpa.

The doctor advised a C-section in hour seven of labor, and half of me wanted to make it to twelve—like the twelve labors of Hercules, you know—but I was exhausted and there was pain unfurling at the base of my spine and so they put me under. What a funny phrase; to be "put under." Anyways. That's what they did. And then they cut me open.

And then they put my baby boy in my arms, this small, red wrinkly thing that I made— he wasn't mine. Didn't feel like mine. He yawned, eyes blinking open and it felt like he could see me, was looking straight through me. Like he knew too much already, this strange small thing in my arms. I shifted him in my arms, laid a hand to my stomach, all tender flesh and loose skin. He gasped a little, a tiny concerned noise that sounded just like my mother. But he wasn't mine. Not mine.

. . . .

I'm back in our apartment now, in our bedroom with the filmy blue curtains my mom brought back from a trip to France, and the chestnut dressing table that Robert's grandfather made for me when we got married. It's been three weeks, I think, since the white room. I called the doctor yesterday. I wanted to know if it was possible for an epidural to have residual effects. The numbness hasn't worn off. He said to just take it slow, recommended me a few new mother therapy groups at the hospital and I hung up halfway through because his voice made me itchy and he was talking for too long anyways.

I feel hollow. They carved me open and stitched me back together and I feel like a nesting doll, echoing and empty, all my other parts orphaned.

There is a cry from somewhere near my bed, a dissonant, cruel sound and I press my hand against my stomach—*protect the baby, protect the baby*—but my stomach is soft, flattened, deflated. There's nothing there. I keep forgetting. I have to remember. Nothing there. Robert comes in and scoops the baby up—not the baby; Cole, Donghai, he has names, I have to remember—and asks me if I want to hold him and I don't, not really, but I want Robert to smile again so I stretch out my arms and he puts the baby in my arms and I bounce him experimentally in my lap. He gurgles.

God, I want a peach.

Robert takes the baby back to feed him, and asks me if I'd like lunch, but I'm not hungry, really. Just tired and the walls are too bright but it's too much to step outside and the hours have started to fade into each other, Monday into Tuesday into Friday.

. . . .

Sometimes I can tell what day it is just by looking out the window. The woman in the apartment just across the courtyard hangs out her delicates to dry, practical sports bras and day of the week underwear every day except for Saturdays like today, when red lace hangs from the window instead, a garish crimson swoop against the mirrored glass.

I had this dress once, in fifth grade. It was the kind of polyester that feels like silk to a five-year old, cream with ruffled sleeves and embroidered roses tumbling across the skirt. I wore it every Wednesday, and every Wednesday felt like a special occasion. When I pulled it out again the next year, for the first day of middle school, the roses were fraying and the dye from the thread had started to fade into the fabric. I wore it anyways, because it made me feel beautiful, special; until Tristan Graber sat behind me and pointed and laughed, said that the dress made me look like I'd gotten my period. "The walking tampon," he called me.

I don't know why I thought of that just now. Maybe it's that red swoop or maybe it's the blood that still speckles the sheets sometimes when I wake up, or the tiny red mulberries in the snow-covered bushes just outside the window.

There is a sharp, screeching sound outside and I pull the curtains back. There are two crows fighting over a mouse carcass in the garden, scrabbling in the dirt until one of them launches into the air, mouse in its beak, and the crows are flying up and up until they are silhouettes against the sun, red-rimmed, swooping shadows. They remind me of the stories that my grandma used to tell me before bed: of the *Jīnwū*, sun-crows that traveled by carriage across the sky, who loved gold, descending from heaven to steal the gilt off funeral pyres and the beads from wedding crowns. One day, they all came to earth at once and set the world on fire, fields turning to ash and castles burning and sand turning to glass.

I nap and dream about the world on fire, about crows coming to roost in our fireplace, nesting in the embers. But my dream, as they all have these days, turns back to the white room. I am back in the hospital and I can hear infomercials in the background and there is a man knocking at the door. Sometimes it is a doctor and sometimes it's our postman and sometimes it's Robert, but sometimes it's Donghai, all grown-up. In these dreams, he looks exactly like the picture of my great-grandfather that my parents have on their mantle: in uniform, hair close-cropped and eyes solemn. In these dreams he holds my hand and he whispers to me in a kind, kind voice that I was never meant to be a mother, that I was barren, that I was toxic. He holds my hand and he kisses my cheek and explains that he's here to save me.

And then he stabs a syringe into my spine and I am numb again, just a mannequin in a bed, nerves extinguished, and he takes the baby from my arms and I didn't even know there was a baby in my hands and I scream and scream and scream—

I wake up tasting peaches and antiseptic.

. . . .

The baby gets sick on a Friday, a fever and a cough that starts in the night, a rasping noise that I mistake for the tiny scritch of rat feet on linoleum. The fever rises with the sun and Robert takes him to the pediatrician's office. It is the first time that I've been alone in the apartment since the hospital, and when I step out of the bedroom, it feels like I've walked into someone else's home. I drift from room to room, tidying the mess of pillows on the couch, the dishes in the sink, the cigarette stubs in the living room ashtray.

I'm in the living room straightening the books when something moves just behind me and I jump, fear sharp and cloying in the back of my throat, ready for a needle against my spine, a nightmare come to life—but it is just the television left on, muted and technicolor, a fight scene from some superhero movie Robert and I had seen in theaters a few months ago. Just the television.

I fall asleep to the sound of airplane engines and gunshots clanging against metal. In my dreams there are bleached sheets and bleached walls and the low hum of machinery and I wait for someone to come. Someone always comes—and there he is, Donghai, my beautiful boy, creeping in through the door, just in time. He holds my hand and he says he's come for a bedtime story and his eyes are just like mine, just like looking into a mirror, and I wait for them to come, the whispers. But for the first time he doesn't speak: just sits and twines his fingers in mine, and the silence is a pressure that grows so loud against my temples that I open my mouth to scream—

And he smiles beatifically and there is the prick of a needle at the base of my neck and just before the pain, just for a moment, the syringe feels like waking up and learning how to breathe and feel and want again.

Like guilt and sorrow and summer-sweet peaches.

I wake up to damp cheeks and the slam of the front door. Robert says my name. I hear him kicking off his shoes and the baby babbling and it feels wrong, all wrong. Like the world cracked and then shifted back into place but not quite right. Not right.

I wrap myself deeper into the blankets and close my eyes: pretend that I'm asleep, that I'm not here, that I'm in a bleachbright room waiting for a door to open.

. . . .

Robert goes back to work on Monday so I put on my bathrobe to take out the garbage. I can't find my shoes so I put on Robert's sneakers. They look like clown shoes on me, floppy and wide, and I stand at the dumpster for a minute, wondering what I look like, what my coworkers would say if they saw me standing with two plastic bags in a bathrobe and overlarge shoes, in a garbage-strewn alleyway. I wonder if it matters.

We moved my grandmother to a nursing home when I was sixteen because she had started wandering the streets at night. I'd apologized when we left, busying my hands with the pillows on the couch.

"Dad says it's just that someone might think that you're dangerous."

"I'm not," she'd replied absently, running a hand across her new couch. "I'm just searching." She hummed disapprovingly. "The flowers on this couch are too itchy." Her nails had caught on the embroidery and when I reached out to pull at the loose strings, she hid her hands behind her back and looked at me embarrassedly, guiltily.

My grandmother had been a concert pianist for years, and even as she'd gotten older, she'd been proud of her hands: long-fingered, graceful, always manicured. The nail-biting had started just before the wandering, just another thing the doctors diagnosed as a symptom and my parents diagnosed as grief. I knew that if I'd reached for her hands, I'd find nails torn to the quick, skin raw and wind-chafed.

She'd reached for me, before I left. "You look like your mom, sweetheart. You wear your sadness on your face, just like her. Just like me." She'd cupped my chin in shaking hands, voice forlorn. "You wear it just like me."

I think of her as I tighten the belt of my bathrobe: of her and the flowers on that couch and what it means to wear sadness. As I straighten to throw the bags into the dumpster, I see a man just out of the corner of my eye: tall and uniform-clad, shifting in the back of the alleyway. I feel a familiar sharp prick on the back of my neck, a desperate hope that it is Donghai—but when I turn, he's gone. Resignation settles into my lungs, cotton-dry and choking. He was a trick of the light, I suppose. A mirage.

. . . .

I think that I'd like to go back to work soon. We've found a good nursery school for the baby, and it's getting easier and easier to look at him in the cradle, playing with his toes or gnawing on a toy—he's teething, I think—or chattering to himself in gibberish.

When I dream, it's almost always Donghai at the door now, and sometimes he takes the baby from my arms but sometimes I wake up before that happens, wake up with the memory of warm weight in my arms and that powdery-sweet baby smell, and the faint taste of peaches fuzzy on my teeth.

I wrote this paper once, for a political science class in college, in which I used Brutus's speech from *Julius Caesar*—the one everyone thinks of when they think of the play; you know, "There is a tide in the affairs of men, that when taken at the flood…"—and used it as a framework through which to discuss Chinese immigration and transpacific trade to Shanghai during the Gold Rush. I titled it "The Specific Ocean." When he returned it, my teacher had crossed out "Specific" and had written "Pacific" next to it with a smiley face, and for a moment I'd thought that maybe "Pacific" was a word he was using to describe that smiley face, placid and aimless and grinning. But I knew he'd written "Pacific" because he thought it had been an accidental slip: an issue of language barriers, just faulty phonetics.

I'd meant the specific ocean: the specific ocean I was born next to, blue and immense and echoing, the specific ocean that buoyed me the first time I learned to swim. The specific ocean that lay between San Francisco and the glittering city where my parents grew up. But I didn't say anything. I just went home and tacked it up on the wall and reminded myself that I was living in someone else's specifics.

I've been wondering if I don't recognize the baby because we've given him too many names. Too many people to be when he grows up, and too few ways to be himself. Pacificity and not specificity.

I don't know. I've been a little scattered lately.

I'm going back to work tomorrow though, and baby is gurgling away in his crib and things are not so bad, I'm not doing so bad.

Robert will be home soon, with the baby, and we can go try that new restaurant that our neighbors recommended, the pizza place near Sixth Street—

I'm sorry. I just, I think I hear someone knocking.

There's a man at the door.

I should go.

THREE

ON YOUR TENTH BIRTHDAY, YOUR family's refrigerator stops working. There is an ice cream cake on the top shelf, with perfect frosting roses and a glossy circle of raspberry syrup, and it melts into an oozing mess, sticky and garishly pink, dripping indiscriminately onto onions and week-old bread and broccoli.

Your mom puts candles in Girl Scout cookies instead, tall stacks of trefoils and thin mints. A delivery truck arrives at your door four days later with a new fridge, just as your dad is leaving for Ireland—a physics conference that you secretly think might be a spy convention. He signs the delivery form and the UPS woman rolls it into your foyer, the moving cart rattling with the weight of the box. Your dad pretends to pick up a phone and makes a joke about the refrigerator running, and you roll your eyes because you're ten now, double digits, and your dad is just such a dad.

After he's gone, the front door locked behind him, you and your mom unwrap the refrigerator, layers of bubble wrap and Styrofoam drifting to your feet. Lyddie laughs, kicking the bits of foam into the air, little white clusters that flutter down like snow. Your mom uncovers the instructions from the debris and you sit on the floor together as she shows you how to screw in the door handles and assemble the crisper drawer. Her voice is soothing, assured, and it feels like she's installed a hundred refrigerators before but when you ask her she just laughs and shakes her head.

"I just have a lot of experience following manuals," she says, switching your grip on the screwdriver.

Your parents have been such a unit your entire life that it's only in moments like this that you remember that your mom made her own way first. Three waitressing jobs and graduate school and living alone in that shoebox apartment on 3rd and Elm, learning to drive, making enough money to pay for a plane ticket and the first six months of your dad's Ph.D. program.

The fridge burbles when it turns on, settling into a comforting hum that you didn't realize you'd missed in the white noise of your house. Your mom flops onto the floor, a little breathless from pushing the refrigerator to its nook by the oven. Lyddie sits on her stomach and you throw your arms around both of them, a tangle of limbs and laughter. She props her chin on top of Lyddie's head to look at you.

"What do you say to a girls' night out?" She smiles, wide and bright, and you think to yourself that your mom is the prettiest person in the world. "Out to the grocery store? We've got no food in the house."

It's snowing again when you pull onto the road, frost lacing the edges of the windshield.

You suck in a breath, the air inside the car still frigid, heavy with the scent of the clove cigarettes that your mom likes to smoke when she's driving on her own. The air is candy-sweet and sharp against your tongue, like Froot Loops and ice, and you cough. The heat turns on with a staticky hum, and you press your cheek against the window, the handle of the door pressed against your ribcage. Lyddie hums a song from *The Sound of Music*, the one they sing to learn the scales, swinging her feet against back of the front seat.

Thump. Thump. Thump.

"Lyddie?" Your mom says lightly. "Could you stop that for a little bit? I just need to focus."

"On what?"

"On the roads, honey."

"But why?"

"Because of the snow." You hear the tension creep into your mom's voice, and so you turn to Lyddie and ask her to explain the very complicated rules involved in her most recent play date adventure, "Mermaids versus Griffins." Under the lamplight outside, the streets are dark and slick, the car catching the wind at right turns. When your mom pulls in front of the grocery store, her hands are shaking. You slip a mittened hand through hers in the freezer aisle, squeezing once.

"Are you okay?"

She squeezes you back. "Just fine."

Lyddie sprints towards the two of you, scarf flying behind her, a tub of ice cream in hand. Your mom laughs and swoops Lyddie up to smack a kiss against her cheek, asking her if she can find cake mix too—

For your tenth-plus-four-days birthday, you get a new fridge and an ice cream cake and the assurance that your mom is braver than anyone else in the world.

SO YOU WANT TO BE A WORKING
WOMAN (INSTRUCTIONS INCLUDED)

LAND AN INTERVIEW: AT A magazine, a law firm, an insurance company, the new wing at the hospital. Schedule it for two weeks out—after your background checks have cleared and they've had the chance to get more information sorted about the position: title and benefits and reporting staff, they explain. The boring legal trimmings.

Hang up and call your parents as you click through information about the company. Commit names to memory: the president, the head of your department, the board of directors. Ask your mom if you should negotiate your salary. Laugh when she tells you not to count your chickens before they're hatched, or not to put all your eggs in one basket, not to put the wagon before the horse, or some other bit of proverb she picked up from late night PBS reruns.

Bring a notebook with you everywhere, to jot down questions to ask your interviewer: ones that'll make you seem interested, not desperate; informed, not a know-it-all; professional, not aloof. Remind yourself not to talk too much, not to bulldoze, not to be a "bossy bee" like your kindergarten teacher Ms. Winchester used to call you, when you told Jimmy Fischer to give you your crayons back.

Put a pair of Louboutins on hold at Saks. The black ankle boots, or the nude pumps, or the navy wedges: something neutral, that goes with everything. Smooth out the creases in your suit jackets, hang your silk shirts in the bathroom so the wrinkles dissipate when you shower. Like steam cleaning, but cheaper. Call your mom again and ask her if you should buy the boots or the pumps, if you should wear a skirt or slacks, if you should wear your hair up or down. Send her pictures of yourself in the mirror; give her options. The navy sheath dress with your hair half-pulled back. The bow-back suit and red heels that your college roommate called your "Dorothy-out-of-Oz" outfit. When she tells you that appearances aren't everything, let her finish: don't judge a book by its cover, all that glitters is not gold, beauty is in the eye of the beholder. Laugh and tell her you love her, say hi to dad, I've got to go now. Hang up.

Meet your sister in the tea parlor at Saks, the one where you had all of your birthday parties until you were sixteen. Tell her about the interview as she stacks tea sandwiches in neat Jenga towers on your plate. Ask her how she is: the new apartment, medical school, the foray into vegetarianism. Eat her salmon sandwiches and save her the raspberry scones and laugh when she drops cheesecake down her shirt. Feel brighter.

Wander through the aisles arm-in-arm, like when you were younger and the store was a maze. Buy a dove-grey cashmere twinset, because your sister tells you that the cream is a little "mother-of-the-bride." At home, put it on again and twist your hair into a chignon, the one you've been practicing since you were thirteen and first saw Audrey Hepburn in *Roman Holiday*: a sleek knot low on your neck, a few strands of hair pulled out to rest against the curve of your cheek. Look at yourself in the mirror and practice introducing yourself: it's so nice to be here. I'm so grateful for the opportunity. My name is, I've worked at, I really think that I can leverage my skill set in this role—be gracious and engaged and personable.

When your interviewer tells you you're a "very lovely young lady," or that it'll be "good to have some female energy in this office," or "you'll pretty up the space in no time, no doubt," smile and nod and bite your tongue. Sign the contract and get your badge printed and go to HR to fill out the paperwork and don't make a fuss. Clean out your purse for your first day of work, with old receipts and brochures and folded-up Band-Aids gathered at the bottom. Empty one of the inside pockets and find old Pier 1 furniture coupons and paint samples, a neatly creased list of job postings, a crumpled stack of apartment listings. The detritus of new beginnings.

Settle into your new beginnings. Be competent and thorough, never ask for too much, remind yourself that success is sacrifice. You can't make an omelette without breaking some eggs.

Overhear someone call you a bitch after your first big presentation. Think of that afternoon in middle school when you refused to kiss Danny Mason during spin-the-bottle, or the first month after you tested into the senior calculus class as a ninth grader, or when you were seventeen and you accidentally cut someone off on the freeway. Tell yourself you've learned not to make mountains out of molehills.

Call your parents. Tell them about the new job, how much you like your coworkers, the family pictures that you have up in your cubicle: your family at Disney, or the National Zoo, or cliffside at the Grand Canyon, your smile gap-toothed and wide. At your department happy hour, when your boss tells you that he hopes he'll see you in his office more, his door is wide open; that you look thirsty or that you have beautiful hands—

Make a bad joke about "clear eyes, open doors, can't lose," and excuse yourself to the bathroom; or tilt your wine glass in his direction and clear your throat, all set, but thanks. Smile politely, look at your hands, slim and tan against the marble countertop. They are your father's hands: too feminine for his body, your grandmother had said, on days that she was trying to be cruel. Too feminine.

Go on dates with men you meet at mixers for young profes-
sionals: at dimly lit tapas bars or marbled sushi counters or sleek
fusion restaurants specializing in molecular gastronomy. They all
wear Armani cologne and have the same expensive haircut: probably
Fleischmann's Barbershop, you know from some of your coworkers.
They talk to you about potential and workflows and building out
career-changing deals and they buy you cocktails you don't want;
and when you look them in the eye for too long, these corporate
hotshots, they flinch and ask for the check.

Work long hours. Work overtime. Work late nights and early
mornings, weekends and holidays. Call your family every month,
and then every two months, and then let the drift happen because
you're trying to keep everything else together.

Get a Christmas bonus and take your family out for dinner and
when your mom tells you that "no woman is an island," and then
"absence makes the heart grow fonder," you know it's a lecture and
you snap at her, say something about the expressions being trite, your
mom just silly and naive, or you hating expressions where "man" has
to be replaced with "woman," as if women are just substitutes. You've
never seen your parents look at you that way: like a stranger, a threat.

Go home. Work longer hours. Get your first big promotion. Call
your parents—almost. Call your sister instead, and watch a Lifetime
romance called *The Spirit of Christmas*, where the protagonist has to
choose between a man and her career. She is a lawyer/journalist/
corporate-something and the romantic interest is a ghost/vampire/
married man and when she chooses him at the end, turn the TV
off and put the popcorn bowl in the sink and wonder what any of it
had to do with Christmas.

Start seeing a coworker. Meet him by the water cooler; or in the elevator on the way to a meeting; or at the coffee stand on the first floor. Ignore the press of his wedding ring against your clavicle the first time he kisses you. Realize early on his penchant for emphatic social diagnoses.

"This is just a symptom, not the disease!" about the gender pay gap.

"There is just an epidemic of mediocrity among college graduates today," as you eat leftover takeout and page through resumes for summer interns.

Fall in love—not with him, but with the particulate romance of an affair, kaleidoscopic and fragmented; built in memories, not futures. Wonder, three months in, if it is just easier to date a married man. Neater, in ways. Compartmentalized, no commitment attached.

When he tells you that he was a Classics major before business school, ask him to say something for you, anything. He tells you it's a dead language, but then you start getting bits and pieces of Ovid during dinner, Caesar when you're putting on your jacket to go. On the nights he stays over, your limbs tangled in the sheets, in the dark; he rests a hand on your hip and conjugates until one of you falls asleep. *Sum es est, sumus estis sunt.*

End things with him in June. Realize that it feels like breathing again.

When he replies—this is silly, I love you, you love me, we love each other—think of dead languages and conjugations. *Amo amas amat. Amamus amatis amant.*

Leave him in the coffeeshop. See him in the office the next day and nod. Say hello. Move on, easy as pie. Wonder if you should quit your job and write Lifetime scripts about falling out of love with unsuitable men. It seems to be a narrative they're missing.

One of your summer interns puts in a sexual harassment complaint at Human Resources: your boss put his hand on her knee during a meeting; or he came up behind her at her desk and started massaging her shoulders; whatever it is, it doesn't matter, because he gets ten thousand dollars cut from his yearly bonus and she gets fired. And two months later, when he botches a major deal and loses a client and gets transferred—a demotion by all standards—you pull up the intern's information and think about contacting her to tell her. Wonder if it would help or hurt.

Meet your new boss. When she asks you if you're planning on having kids, stutter, because you're twenty-six years old and everyone has prepared you to hear this question but no one has ever prepared you to answer. She tells you that the right answer is no, whatever the truthful answer is. The truthful answer doesn't matter. She tells you that a pause like that could get you fired at certain high-flying commerce and computing companies on the West Coast, her voice cool and clinical but not unkind. Half of you wants to ask her how she got to where she is. The other half of you wants to ask if it ever changes, or if she just had to learn to block it out: the dismissals, the underrating, the white noise of casual harassment.

You think it might be the same question.

Call your mom two nights later, her "hello" guarded and careful, crackling over the line. Tell her you're sorry. Tell her you miss her. And when she replies with "valor is the better part of discretion," say that you don't think that's exactly the expression. Laugh anyways, because it sounds like forgiveness. Turn your work phone off and talk for three hours: about your dad's new kayaking hobby, your sister's graduation, what to make for New Year's dinner if she's well and truly vegetarian. Say hello to your dad and let him read you an excerpt from the article he was reading: something about glaciers in the Pacific or the ethical harvest of coffee beans. Say I love you. Say it twice; mean it. Hang up and go to bed and dream of coffee beans and valor.

And in the office the next morning, when Tom from Marketing asks you why you weren't on call, smile and tell him he'll have the files by noon, it was unreasonable to expect them outside of work hours—and did he know, you learned very recently, valor is the better part of discretion? Feel a little different. Walk a little taller. Wonder if it will last.

FOUR

THE FIRST TIME YOU REALIZE your dad is a romantic, you are in Shanghai for your great-grandfather's funeral. It is the summer after your senior year of high school and you are sitting on the couch, back straight, in a white sheath dress borrowed from your mother.

Your grandma has been cooking for five hours straight: glistening cubes of pork belly, steamed lentils and hard-boiled eggs, stewed tomatoes and eggs, your great-grandfather's favorite dish. The funeral party has congregated in the living room and on the courtyard of her first-floor apartment, the ancestral weight of the family tombs giving way now to family gossip and familial one-upmanship. You are fairly certain that the group near the living room table has gathered because your mom just started arm wrestling her brother. You're proven right when there is a cheer and your mom stands, flushed and victorious. Your dad claps her on the back and she looks up at him, beaming, leaning into his shoulder. Your uncle bows to the crowd, a gallant loser.

It's nice, you think. To have family. When you turn back to her, you realize your grandma is watching your parents too, the spoon in her hand dripping sudsy water onto the floor. She's smiling, and you give her a moment before you clear your throat and she jumps a little before turning back to the stove.

You remember the first time your grandmother told you about the day your parents met: an accidental bicycle accident, your mom on the sidewalk and your dad juggling physics textbooks as he tried to help her up. How he'd said it was love at first sight. You'd called it a "meet-cute" and then had spent a day explaining to your grandmother what exactly a "meet-cute" was.

When your parents come back inside, your dad is explaining something about mechanical energy and kinetics to your mom. Your mom shoots you a familiar look—exasperated, amused, achingly fond—as they start to carry dishes from the kitchen out to the living room. Your dad picks up a bowl of congee and then sets it in the windowsill so that he can show your mom the mathematically-proven ideal angle of impact for an arm wrestling contest. He leaves it there as he follows your mom into the living room, and your grandmother sighs, retrieving the dish.

"You know, your father was so absentminded when he was younger that he'd forget the clothes on his back if he wasn't wearing them," your grandmother says as she starts lifting dumplings from a wok. She's always been prone to talking like this, statements that sound like proverb or allegory until you think about them a little more and realize they're just facts. "Books and numbers were the only things that stuck, until your mom." She waves the spatula towards the living room. "They're all still on the shelves."

You bring the plate of dumplings to the living room and pause to browse the shelves, running your fingers along unfamiliar titles. The top two shelves are all history and physics, from middle school workbooks to college texts. But on the third shelf, tucked between *Theory of Quantum Electrodynamics* and *Relativity: The Special and the General Theory*, you find your mom's graduate thesis: "A Regression Analysis of Non-Linear Eigenstructure Relationships." It is a thin volume, dog-eared and filled with your dad's handwriting: doodles, diagrams, questions, marginal proofs.

Your dad told you once that the reason he was a physicist was that physics felt like discovering all of the ways in which the world was falling in love with itself. You didn't quite understand him until you took your first applied physics class in high school and you learned about spontaneous nuclear fission. You think now that your dad might be a physicist because spontaneous nuclear fission isn't all that different from love at first sight.

You take the book with you back to the kitchen, setting it down next to the stove and resting your chin on your grandmother's shoulder. She turns to press a kiss to your temple and you feel her bones shift beneath your ear.

You used to do this when you were younger, in the months after Lyddie was born and your grandparents came to stay with your family in the states for awhile. You'd rest your head in the crook of her shoulder and she would tell you stories about your parents: their first date, their first fight, the first time they brought you to China. You'd listen to her voice and her breath and her bones until you fell asleep, there on her shoulder, and she'd carry you to bed. "*Ni shi cong ai qing sheng de,*" she'd whisper as she tucked you in. "You were born of love."

She sounds the same, still. She's thinner, frailer, but her voice sounds the same. Her bones sound the same.

ROM-COM (SCENES FROM
THE CUTTING ROOM FLOOR)

FEBRUARY: **IN FEBRUARY, A WELL-MEANING** friend told Lena that Eli was getting married. She was at the grocery store, standing in the cereal aisle and deciding between cornflakes and bran, and her first thought was not of his wedding, or his fiancé, or the earrings that she left on his nightstand, but instead, of cereal boxes.

"Didn't they used to have games on the backs of these?" Lena wondered out loud.

The friend looked at her like she was crazy. "He's getting married two months after you ended things, and you want to talk about cereal boxes?" She put a hand on her shoulder, turning Lena to face her.

I don't care, Lena wanted to say. Things are done, over, finished, kaput. Caring about that would be like caring about a book that has an ending you don't like, or a superhero movie that casts someone who doesn't fit the character, or a puzzle piece that you accidentally vacuumed.

But it felt a little dramatic to say (and she didn't know how to explain it anyways, that she stopped loving him because she stopped wanting to draw him, because he stopped being art—which she felt made her sound at best ridiculous, and at worst, off the rails) so instead, she said that she cared, of course she cared, but she was the one who broke up with him, and she was just happy that he was happy, and besides, she really did wonder why it was that cereal boxes didn't have games on the back anymore.

. . . .

December: When people asked how they met, Lena would tell the story backwards. Eli asked her once if this was because she didn't remember the beginning. He was joking, of course; they'd spent months talking about how they met, sorting through the little details. Because that's what you do when you care about someone, he'd said: you parse and piece and puzzle through the time just before they were yours.

She thought, maybe, that she told the story backwards because she liked to see it unravel, liked to give her audience the distance that they were going to travel before they actually did it. Because if she told it backwards, it felt less like her own story and more like she was watching characters unfold.

. . . .

October: Eli went to bed at ten every night, and Lena got in the habit of crawling into the sheets next to him just as he was falling asleep, turning on old *Cheers* reruns and muting them, mouthing the words to herself as she worked on lesson plans and sketches for class. The reruns ended just after midnight, but she always left the TV on to watch the commercials that played, for ridiculous things that she'd never see in daylight hours. Toasters that printed patterns onto your bread. Back scratchers shaped like cats. Nightlights that looked like candles, and turned off when you blew on them. They were almost grotesquely fascinating to her, these commercials for things that someone, somewhere must be buying. Useless things. Late night things.

She wondered about the other people in the world who might be watching the same images scatter across their screens, pictured a map of the world and red lines spiderwebbed across it, connecting all of them; the dim bedrooms and insomnia-ridden nights threaded together.

The light of the television screen glimmered, blue and fluorescent and rippling across the grey cotton of her bedspread. At one in the morning, without fail, the streetlight next to her window would sputter and go out. Sometimes, with a long creaking sigh, Eli would shift to wrap his arm across her hip, thumb hooked in the curve of her hipbone, whispering an "I love you" into her stomach. Sometimes she'd say it back. Sometimes, she'd pretend she hadn't heard him.

. . . .

September. Two months after she and Eli started seeing each other, a boy drowned at the pier near the lighthouse. Lena had never met him, Will Loyola, but his brother was one of her favorite students, always the first to get to the studio and the last to leave. She spent September watching as he fragmented, as his paintings fractured and sharpened with the concision of sorrow. She felt helpless and tired and painfully, guiltily, seethingly jealous when she saw his art.

She went to the memorial service. It was on the beach, the tides creeping up the shoreline, still and quiet and humid. She watched the water lap at her toes and she wondered absently, with clinical curiosity, what it would be like to drown: water feathered against your skin, across your spine, seeping into your lungs with careless intimacy. The compression of breath just before sinking, crystalline and suspended. The letting go.

The lighthouse was bright against the sky that night, a sun-bleached pillar on the rocky side of the beach, stretching up, stark and accusatory in the moonlight. There was an abandoned lifeboat near the lighthouse, one of the cheap inflatable ones that you could get at any Big Mart. It was sagging and deflated, listless against the sand, and she couldn't stop staring at it, even as the service began. Eli was standing next to her, fingers woven loosely in hers, tealight in his other hand. A drop of wax dripped onto his wrist and he didn't even flinch, just let go of her hand briefly to pull it off his skin.

People stepped forward to slip their candles into the water, their feet sending billows of sand into the air, candlelight filtering through in slim gilt strands. The Loyolas stepped forward with an urn, dark and unvarnished, and scattered Will's ashes along the shoreline. The wind blew the ash back a little, tangling with the sand around Lena's feet. A few people leapt back to avoid it, and somewhere behind her, a small child asked his mother if the beach was made of zombie dust and dead people. His mom hushed him, but the boy's voice stayed in her mind even as Eli slid a gentle hand across her back, and people began to disperse. The sand was all hills and valleys where people had been standing, but she could see the tide coming in, sweeping the beach clean.

For a brief moment, she was reminded of a whale carcass that had washed ashore a few summers before, the stale, cloying odor of decaying flesh that had cloaked the beach for days. It had rotted from the inside out, nature dismantling it with vicious effectiveness. Two weeks after the whale carcass had been removed, she'd returned to the spot on the beach where it'd laid. She hadn't expected much, but she'd expected something: a dip in the sand from the weight, a barren circle, dark and fecal. Instead, she'd found swooping seagulls, sun-gilded sand, and a child's birthday party: streamers and candles and cake. As if it'd never happened.

Eli reached for her hand and asked if she was ready to go. His face was open, kind and gentle.

For a moment, she resented him—just a little.

. . . .

August: She liked Eli because he was sweet and thoughtful, but really because when they first met, her hands itched to draw him, to map the sharp angles of his cheekbones, to smudge charcoal shadows across his shoulder blades.

He started to say "you and me, all the way down to the end of the line," a few weeks into dating, and she cringed every time he said it, because it sounded infinite and romantic and exaggerated in a way that made her itchy, like her skin was too tight and the world was too small. Then she saw *Double Indemnity*, black and white and grainy, Fred MacMurray at his stone-faced finest, and she realized that the end of the line wasn't a promise of forever, but an execution sentence for two characters who only loved each other when they were lying.

Somehow, it made her like him just a little better.

. . . .

June: The morning was grey-stained and damp the day they met. It was summer, and for weeks, the nights had been bright with heat lightning. The cottonwood seeds that month came in lilting waves so thick that people mistook them for snow falling outside their windows: sheets of them, in pollen-ridden dust clouds, hanging low on the eaves of houses, seeping into the cracks in the sidewalk, collecting in tree leaves and sliding through Lena's hair. It dusted the tables at her favorite diner, piled in soft drifts near the curb, got caught in windshield wipers and stuck in mailboxes, made the air feel like grit and cotton, setting everyone a little on edge.

She had broken her pinky toe earlier that week, but hadn't gone to the doctor yet, had just kept walking on it, the skin just under the nail turning all sorts of interesting colors: purples and greens and a sickly yellow at the edges. The bruise blended in with the paint splattered up and down her legs, from the mural that she was painting for the school gymnasium. She was working part-time, too, at the local print shop, and her hands were perpetually tattooed with the ghosts of words: *just in, all new* across her palm; DEALS DEALS DEALS a ring around her thumb; stray letters tucked in the hollow of her wrist.

She was leaning against the checkout counter at the library, chin braced on a stack of books, when she dropped her library card and stopped to pick it up. Her books, balanced precariously against her cheek, wobbled and tumbled to the ground. She heaved a sigh and collected them from the floor, slid them one by one into the return bin, kneeling on the Formica-tiled floor of the lobby. Bracing her hands on her thighs, she stood, just as she heard a voice to her left.

"Excuse me, I think you dropped this."

It was the perfect meet-cute movie moment.

FIVE

Everything is routine until it's not.

Your mom goes in for a checkup. It is November 14th. Her doctor finds a lump in her breast and orders a mammogram—

Protocol, just to check in and make sure anything we find is benign; there's only an 8% chance that you'll need to get a biopsy.

And then four days later your mom gets a biopsy—

There's only a 2% chance that the tumor is malignant, but we just want to make sure—

And then five days later the doctor calls and it's the first day that you start to think of your mom as a statistic: as a set of chances, of numbers.

. . . .

Everything is routine until it's not.

You've all been coping in your own way. Lyddie throws herself into her schoolwork— into early mornings and late nights and extra credit assignments until you've forgotten what classes she's enrolled in because it feels like she's just taking all of them. Your dad spends every waking hour researching, calling oncologists in other states, comparing treatment centers, poring over MRIs with a magnifying glass. One day you walk into his office and find that his medical texts have all been replaced with cookbooks, ones with titles like "Cooking Through Chemo" or "Eat to Beat Cancer." You kiss the top of his head and leave him a cup of tea—he barely notices.

You've all been coping in your own way: so you go back to college. And during the sunlight hours you go to class and you see your friends and you eat your meals and you run and run and run, until your lungs ache and you can't breathe and there is a throbbing pressure behind your temples that blacks out everything else. Blissful, undeserved silence.

At night you wrap yourself in strangers' sheets: dark, quiet heat, hands and teeth and limbs slick with sweat—no talking. Sometimes, in the sooty blue light just before dawn, you wake up and pause for a moment to listen to them breathe: evenly, softly, the air wafting against your back.

In, out. In, out.

You aren't looking for comfort, really. Not platitudes or company or a hand to hold in the dark. You just want a metronome. Someone to remind you how to breathe.

You've all been coping in your own way so you don't ask when the credit cards start coming in: little rectangles in a rainbow assortment of colors, with your mom's name in blocky letters marching across the plastic. She never uses them, not that you can tell; she just tucks them away, one, three, five at a time. A month after her diagnosis, she has ten new credit cards slotted neatly in her wallet.

"I just want things with my name on it," she tells you one night as you're shopping for Christmas gifts online, your feet tucked under her legs. She hands you her wallet and you run your fingers over the letters and numbers, pressing them into the pad of your thumb. "I want open accounts and monthly statements and things left undone." She combs your hair with her fingers, like she used to do when you were young, before your sister was born. "Something to leave behind. Some kind of permanence."

You memorize all of the numbers, a 160-digit sequence that you recite in your head for months after. It is your own kind of permanence.

Everything is routine until it's not.

Your dad drives your mom to every chemotherapy session, every surgery consultation, every radiation treatment. Chemo on Wednesdays, and new MRIs every two weeks. Radiation on Thursdays and two hours with the will and the financial planner every Friday afternoon, because even cancer can't break habits, and your parents are always prepared for the "just in case."

Your mom's progress with chemo slows. They increase her dosage. Your phone tells you that your "most-used" words are "home" and "mastectomy." At school, in your senior seminar, you read a short story about a mother watching her child go through chemotherapy. You think you should grieve, but instead there is a bone-deep, vindictive comfort that you find in it, in this assurance that things could be reversed. That maybe there is a world in which you could do this for your mother—live this instead of your mother.

You go home when your mom has complications during her last treatment, take Lyddie out for pancakes after you find her playing Pokemon Go by the vending machines in the ICU. It's one in the morning and you sit in a booth at IHOP, side by side, sharing a blueberry short stack and hash browns, like you did when you were little and your mom took you after piano lessons. You order a sticky bun on instinct, before you remember that after chemo, your mom tastes copper when she eats sweet things. You send it back, uneaten.

"How are you?"

"She's going to be fine, you know."

"I know."

GENERICS

. . . .

Everything is routine until it's not.

The well-meaning guests that drop by to visit your mom all bring packaged meals, because "I can't imagine any of you want to cook at a time like this." You smile and nod, and you and Lyddie place bets on that week's lasagna-to-meatloaf ratio as you stack another foil-wrapped dish in your freezer. You stop buying produce because the refrigerator is full; and besides, your sister eats at school and your dad eats at the hospital and your mom just doesn't eat, and it does seem a little silly to cook for one.

Your mom gets surgery in May. You work on your grad school applications next to her bed, the nightstand piled high with prescriptions and discarded papers. She helps you practice for interviews and you go on walks together: just to the corner at first, then long and longer until one day you end up two miles away at the grocery store and your mom tells you that she wants ice cream, and "could you go get some broccoli, because we don't have any vegetables in the house?" And you start crying, right there in the freezer aisle, because you are finally seeing the end.

ACKNOWLEDGMENTS

Writing is not—and has never been—a solo endeavor for me, and if I were to thank everyone who has made this collection possible, this section would be longer than the book itself. So I'll just say thank you to Sam for her unfailingly brilliant editorial hand; to Natalie, who made my words clearer and lovelier than I knew they could be; to Justine, for understanding what *Generics* meant to me from the very beginning. To my professors at Carleton College, who taught me to think about power, and structure, and selfhood: the narratives we create and the narratives we live. To my friends, my first and best readers:

AB, for reading the rough drafts, always—

JG, whose approval will always be my gold standard—

EK, for the art on my walls, a built-in cure for writer's block—

EM, whose questions shaped this manuscript—

ES, for all the bits of poetry I've learned I can find in the world—

CM, the first person to imagine these stories could be a book—

WJ, who was there for all the elbows—

AZ, for being my emergency contact, ten states away—

MJ, who has always picked up, every time—

KP, for every step, every pace, every spring morning—

SK, for a friendship full of stardust—

CS, who is a constant reminder that *luminous beings are we, not this crude matter*—

AD, for everything, everything, everything—

And to BT, for believing.

Lastly [finally, mostly, always]—thank you to my family. To my father, who taught me faith and curiosity in equal parts. To my mother, who will always be my favorite storyteller. And to my sister, who teaches me every day about what it means to believe in a brighter and truer world. I am so very lucky.

All my love,

JULIE ZHOU was born in Madison, Wisconsin, and despite a fleeting love affair with New England, has always found her way back to the Midwest. She received her B.A. in English from Carleton College in Minnesota. She currently lives in Minneapolis, where she reads by day (as the program assistant for a community reading grant initiative) and writes by night. Her work has received recognition from *Carve Magazine*, *On She Goes*, *[Pank]*, and a deeply wonderful group of friends and family.